POWER-CRAZY MS WIZ

Terence Blacker has been a full-time writer since 1983. In addition to the best-selling *Ms Wiz* stories, he has written a number of books for children, including *Pride and Penalties* and *Shooting Star* from the Hotshots series, *The Great Denture Adventure*, *Nasty Neighbours/Nice Neighbours* and *Homebird*. *Ms Wiz Spells Trouble*, the first book in the *Ms Wiz* series, was shortlisted for the Children's Book Award 1988 and selected for the Children's Book of the Year 1989.

What the reviewers have said about *Ms Wiz*:

"Every time I pick up a Ms Wiz, I'm totally spellbound... a wonderfully funny and exciting read." *Books for Keeps*

"Hilarious and hysterical." Susan Hill, *Sunday Times*

"Terence Blacker has created a splendid character in the magical Ms Wiz. Enormous fun." *The Scotsman*

"Sparkling zany humour... brilliantly funny." *Children's Books of the Year*

Titles in the Ms Wiz series

Terence Blacker

POWER-CRAZY MS WIZ

Illustrated by Tony Ross

**MACMILLAN
CHILDREN'S BOOKS**

First published 1992 by Piccadilly Press Limited
Published 1993 by Pan Macmillan Children's Books

This edition published 1997 by Macmillan Children's Books
a division of Macmillan Publishers Limited
25 Eccleston Place, London SW1W 9NF
and Basingstoke

Associated companies throughout the world

ISBN 0 330 34872 8

1 3 5 7 9 8 6 4 2

A CIP catalogue record for this book is available from
the British Library.

Phototypeset by Intype London Ltd
Printed by Mackays of Chatham plc, Kent

Acknowledgement

I would like to thank the children of Class 12D, Riverside Primary School, Wallasey, whose idea Ms Wiz PM was the inspiration for this story.

CHAPTER ONE

A Lean, Mean
Peter Harris

It was the first day of the holidays, the fair was in town and the sun shone high in the sky. But for Peter Harris, better known as Podge, it felt like the worst day of his life.

He wandered through the fairground, thinking of the bad news he had received that morning. The Big Dipper loomed up in front of him but he walked on. He heard the screams and laughter of children on the Waltza – he hardly looked at them. Even the candy floss store, which was normally Podge's first stop at the fair, didn't interest him today.

Deep in thought, he found himself standing in front of a small, circular store decked out with plastic toys and goldfish in transparent plastic bags. There was a table in the middle with some wooden cubes on it. A sign on the stall read "GET THE HOOP OVER THE CUBE – TAKE A GOLDFISH HOME!"

"Want a go, son?" The stallholder, a red-faced man whose large stomach stretched his dirty white shirt, held out a hoop.

Podge shook his head. He never won anything. Anyway, he wasn't in the mood.

He was just about to move away when

he noticed that one of the fishes seemed to be looking at him with that wide-eyed help-me expression that Podge's friend Henry Wilson put on when there was a maths test at school. Podge frowned – he didn't want to think of school right now.

"Yes, we'll have a go, please."

Podge turned to see, standing beside him, a girl in torn jeans and a baseball cap. The stallholder gave her a hoop which she passed to Podge.

"No, thanks," said Podge quietly. "I'm useless at throwing things."

"Not today you aren't," said the girl.

Sighing, Podge held the hoop before him and took aim. As he drew his hand back, he was aware of a humming sound all around him. Now where had he heard that before? Concentrating as hard as he could, he let the hoop go.

It moved through the air slowly, like a tiny spacecraft, and hovered over the block, before settling neatly around it.

"Eh?" The stallholder looked at the hoop suspiciously.

"Brilliant throw!" said the girl. "We'll have this goldfish, please." She pointed to the fish which Podge had noticed.

Podge looked at her more closely. She was a bit older than he had thought at first and there was something familiar about her flashing green eyes. "Haven't we met somewhere?" Podge asked.

Without a word, she held up her hand.

On her nails was black nail-varnish.

"Ms Wiz!" Podge smiled for the first time that day. "What are you doing here?"

"You know how it is," said Ms Wiz quietly. "I go wherever magic is needed."

Grumpily, the stallholder handed her the goldfish. "Magic," he muttered. "Looked like good old-fashioned cheating to me."

Ms Wiz put her arm around Podge's shoulders. "So," she said. "Tell me your problem."

"I thought you knew everything," said Podge, turning away from the stall. Ms Wiz followed, holding the goldfish in front of her.

"Not everything," she said. "The message I received this morning was 'MAGIC ALERT – PODGE HARRIS – PARENT PROBLEM'."

"*Major* parent problem," said Podge gloomily. "I'm not sure I really want to talk about it."

Ms Wiz walked into a video arcade

and stood in front of a computer game. "When did the problem take place?" she asked.

"This morning at breakfast."

"And your address is . . . ?"

"15 Rylett Road."

Ms Wiz pressed a few buttons on the machine. Briefly the screen went fuzzy and made a quiet humming sound. Then it cleared to show a modern kitchen. In the centre of the room was a table on either side of which sat a man and a woman, looking very serious. Between them was a child, eating.

"Hey, that's me!" Podge gasped. "That's my kitchen! And there's Mum and Dad!"

"It's a magical reconstruction of your kitchen at breakfast this morning. It's going to show me what happened."

"Oh no." Podge winced. "This is going to be really embarrassing."

*

On the screen, the figures started talking.

"Now Peter, we need to have a serious discussion," Podge's father, Mr Harris, was saying.

"Voff avout?" said Podge.

"*Don't* talk with your mouth full," Mr Harris snapped.

"Podge swallowed. "Sorry," he said.

"Today's the start of your holidays, Peter," his father continued. "And from now on there are going to be some changes around here."

"Changes?"

"Number one, you're going to spend less time with your nose in a book, reading stories, and more time learning for exams."

"But—"

"Number two, you're going on a diet. You look like a football on legs. So it's no more chocolate biscuits. This time next month I want to see a lean, mean Peter Harris."

"Lean? Mean?"

"Number three." Mr Harris paused. "I'm taking you away from that school of yours."

Podge gasped.

"St Barnabas." Mr Harris spat the words out in disgust. "All you get there is . . . larking about."

"What about my friends?" Podge protested.

"There'll be time enough for friends when you've passed a few exams," said Mr Harris, getting to his feet. "My decision's final and I won't budge. Will I, Mother?"

"No," Mrs Harris had sighed wearily. "You won't budge."

"Hmm, I see the problem now," said Ms Wiz, as the images faded from the screen. "Somehow we've got to make your father change his mind."

"Some hope," Podge muttered. "You'd

have to be Prime Minister to make my dad change his mind."

"Hey, great vid!" said a voice behind them. Ms Wiz and Podge turned to see Jack Beddows, Podge's best friend. "What did you have to do to win?" said Jack, looking at the screen. "Get the big boy through the kitchen door?"

"Great joke," said Podge.

"I saw you with Ms Wiz," said Jack. "I thought you were playing a game."

"That was no game," said Ms Wiz. "It was real – Podge is being taken away from St Barnabas. It's time for action." She walked out of the video arcade in the direction of the dodgem cars.

"I don't believe it," Jack said to Podge.

"And I'm being put on a diet," said Podge. "My dad says I look like a football on legs. That's not true, is it?"

"Er, well—"

Fortunately for Jack, they were interrupted by Ms Wiz waving to them from a purple dodgem car. "Come on," she shouted. "We've got no time to lose."

"Typical Ms Wiz," said Podge. "It's the most serious day of my life and she wants to ride a bumper car."

Both of them squeezed into the dodgem, with Podge in the driving seat.

"I say." A man eating some candy floss nearby pointed to the dodgem car. "You're only allowed two people per car, you know. I think one of you really ought to get out."

"Do you?" said Ms Wiz innocently.

As the man walked towards a fairground assistant, the candy floss he was holding seemed to be growing larger and larger until, seconds later, it covered the whole of his head and the top of his body.

"Help!" he shouted in a muffled voice. "Where am I? Everything's gone pink."

"Let's go," said Ms Wiz. She reached under her seat and took out a white umbrella which she fixed to the front of the dodgem. It began to turn, faster and faster, like the propeller of a helicopter.

"Er, no, Ms Wiz," said Podge nervously as the dodgem floated upwards. "I don't think this is one of your better ideas."

But the dodgem seemed to have a life of its own. It climbed higher and higher over the fairground.

"Brilliant ride," said Jack. "And we didn't even pay."

"I hate heights!" Podge was clinging on to the steering wheel. "I get travel-sick. This is meant to be a bumper car, not a bumper plane."

As the dodgem picked up speed, Ms Wiz took off her baseball cap and let the wind blow through her long, dark hair. "London, here we come."

"Why are we going to London?" Jack asked.

"Didn't I tell you?" Ms Wiz raised her voice above the whistling of the wind.

"We're off to see the Prime Minister. It was Podge's idea."

"*What?*" said Podge. "I never—"

"Well done, Podge," shouted Jack.

CHAPTER TWO

Mad Goldfish Disease

A purple dodgem car, suspended by a whirling white umbrella, flew high over the streets of London.

As it skimmed a few feet above Buckingham Palace, it seemed to be slowing down.

"Now here's what we're going to do," said Ms Wiz to Podge and Jack. "In a few moments' time, we shall be meeting the Prime Minister—"

"Yeah yeah," muttered Jack who didn't believe anything until he could see it.

"—and I shall be asking him to pass a new law to prevent parents taking children away from schools against their wishes."

"Are you sure he can pass laws all by himself?" asked Podge.

"Of course he can," said Ms Wiz. "He's Prime Minister, isn't he?"

"I think it may be a bit more complicated than that," said Jack.

"Honestly, you two!" Ms Wiz crossed her arms, almost crushing the goldfish she was carrying. "You're so . . . negative. Just trust me."

"We'll have to," said Jack, looking over the edge of the dodgem. "We're coming in to land."

"Now it's very important that we act as a team," said Ms Wiz. "I'll be in charge, Podge will be my adviser and Jack will look after Henry?"

"Henry?"

"Named after Henry Wilson at school," said Podge.

Ms Wiz passed Jack the bag containing the goldfish. "This is Henry," she smiled. "He's very important."

"Typical," grumbled Jack. "Ms Wiz gets the power, Podge gets the fun and I get the goldfish."

The dodgem hovered a few feet above a wide pavement. As it landed, a small crowd of people gathered on the pavement, staring and pointing.

A tall, bearded policeman pushed his way towards them. Taking one look at the dodgem, he reached into his top pocket for a notebook. "No number plates," he muttered to himself. "Parked in a bus lane. Driver under age."

17

Ms Wiz stepped out of the dodgem and Podge noticed that, while they had been travelling, her clothes had changed from a torn T-shirt to a smart grey suit. "I'm sorry about our parking, officer," she said. "We had to stop here because we're looking for an animal hospital."

"Oh yeah?" The policeman drew himself up to his full height. "I don't see no animals."

Without a word, Ms Wiz took the bag containing Henry the goldfish from Jack.

"Look at him, the poor little creature." She held the bag in front of the policeman's face. "He's suffering from Mad Goldfish Disease. Swimming round and round – going bonkers before your very eyes."

"Don't be daft, lady," said the policeman, his eyes following Henry. "All goldfish do that."

"But they don't do this," said Ms Wiz

under her breath, as a distant humming
noise could be heard. "You are now feeling
very . . . drowsy," she said. "You want . . .
to . . . go . . . to . . . sleep."

"I don't believe it," whispered Jack.
"She's using Henry to hypnotise the
policeman."

Slowly Ms Wiz lowered the bag. The
policeman continued to stare into space, his
mouth hanging open.

"You are now under my spell," said Ms

Wiz quietly. "You will do everything you are told. Do you understand?"

"Yes, ma'am," said the policeman.

"Please take me to the Prime Minister's house."

"Yes, ma'am."

"Then come back and make sure no one touches our dodgem."

"No, ma'am. I mean, yes, ma'am."

The policeman turned and slowly, like a sleepwalker, made his way past a barrier and into a quiet side road.

"It's Downing Street," whispered Podge, who had seen a street sign. "This is where the Prime Minister lives."

The policeman reached Number Ten, Downing Street and knocked on the door. "Who shall I say is calling, Ma'am?" he asked.

"Ms Wisdom, Mr Peter Harris and Mr Jack Beddows," said Ms Wiz.

A young woman with neat blonde hair and a neat blue suit opened the door.

"Ms Beddows, Mr Jack Peters and Mr Wisdom Harris to see the Prime Minister," said the policeman in a distant voice.

"Great memory," Jack muttered.

"I'm afraid the Prime Minister is too busy to see anyone but—"

"Too busy?" Ms Wiz pushed forward. "This is important. What's he doing?"

"He's just . . . busy," said the woman, her smile becoming less friendly. "The country doesn't just run itself, you know. Now, my name's Marjorie and I'm from the Prime Minister's office – I'm sure I can help you."

"I don't think so," said Ms Wiz. "This is a highly confidential matter."

"Then in that case, I suggest you write a letter and . . . and . . ." As a faint hum could be heard, Marjorie stopped speaking and stood as motionlessly as if she had been frozen.

"Sorry, Marje," said Ms Wiz, stepping past her into the house. "I'll just have to put a statue spell on you for the moment."

Jack looked nervously at Podge. "I've never seen her this determined," he muttered, as they followed her into the house.

"Now," said Ms Wiz, looking around the dark hall of Number Ten, Downing Street, "I wonder where the person in charge is."

"Why, that must be me."

A man in a dark suit stood at the foot of the stairs in front of them. "Would you mind telling me what you're doing in my house?" he said.

Podge gulped. "It's the P-P-Prime—"

"He looks smaller than he does on telly," said Jack.

Ms Wiz smiled politely. "Marjorie told us you were too busy to see us."

"She was right," said the Prime Minister.

"And we have a problem," said Ms Wiz, extending her hand backwards towards Jack. "He's called Henry."

"Henry?"

"Yes." Ms Wiz held the plastic bag before

the Prime Minister's eyes. "Just look at him." Henry swam round and round and round . . . "You want to go . . . to . . . sleep."

"Why—" The Prime Minister swayed slightly as he spoke in a distant voice. "Why it's a . . . goldfish."

"Prime Minister," said Ms Wiz. "You are now in my power."

CHAPTER THREE
Order! Order!

At 15 Rylett Road, Podge's father Cuthbert Harris was crouched over a pile of wood with a screwdriver in his hand.

"This new desk I've bought will be a surprise for the lad," he was saying to Mrs Harris, who watched him as he tried to make sense of the instructions. "It shows that we're doing our bit. He works harder, loses his story books, goes on a diet, gives up chocolate biscuits, says goodbye to his friends and leaves his school, we buy him a desk. That's fair, isn't it?" He frowned. "Now I wonder how this leg goes."

Without a word, Mrs Harris took the screwdriver from her husband and began to assemble the desk.

"Action, that's the thing," said Mr Harris, leaning against the wall. "In this

life, there are doers and watchers. I want
our lad to do things – like his father."

"Pass me that screw, will you, Cuthbert,"
said Mrs Harris, who was already on the
second leg of the desk.

"The lad's got to learn. It's dog-eat-dog
out there."

"Talking of learning—" Mrs Harris
reached for the third leg "—why have you
taken Peter's books from his shelves?"

"I'm chucking them out," said Mr

Harris. "They're just stories. Those bookshelves will be needed for the exam guides I've bought." He reached inside a plastic bag beside him. "There's *Mathematics for Exams, Geography for Exams, English for Exams*." He opened one of the books.

Mrs Harris picked up the fourth leg of the desk.

"Listen to this, Mother." Mr Harris stabbed a fat finger at the book in his hand.

"It says here, 'Welcome to *English for Exams*. This little guide will help you pass your English tests. The most important thing to remember is that the more books you read, the better you'll be at English.' " Mr Harris frowned, then continued, " 'It doesn't matter what books you read so long as you enjoy . . .' " His voice trailed off.

"Interesting." Mrs Harris smiled to herself as she screwed in the desk's last leg.

"Oh, all right." Podge's father shrugged impatiently. "I suppose Peter can keep his books if he likes."

Mrs Harris stood up and looked at her work with satisfaction. "I wonder where he's got to?" she said.

At that moment, Podge was sitting between Ms Wiz and Jack at a long, shiny table in the Cabinet Room at Number Ten, Downing Street. Facing them was the Prime Minister.

"So that's our problem, Prime

Minister," Ms Wiz was saying. "All we
need you to do is pass a law that will
prevent Mr Harris taking Podge away from
St Barnabas."

The Prime Minister smiled. "I'm glad you
raised that point," he said. "But, at the
end of the day, we're not playing on a level
playing-field. Someone has moved the goal-
posts. We're in a whole different ballgame."

"I beg your pardon?" Ms Wiz looked confused.

"Don't panic, Ms Wiz," said Jack quietly. "This is just the way politicians talk. You have to ask the question again."

"Can you please help us, Prime Minister?"

"That's a very good question," said the Prime Minister. "But, as I've said on a number of occasions, there's a whole range of options and—"

Ms Wiz banged the table. "Yes or no, PM?"

"Er . . . no."

"Why not?" Podge asked. "You're meant to be the person in charge."

"Parliament," said the Prime Minister. "Laws have to go through Parliament."

For a moment there was silence in the Cabinet Room. "That's it then," said Podge eventually. "Not even Ms Wiz could hynotise the whole of Parliament."

"Unless . . ." An odd smile had appeared on the Prime Minister's face. "Unless someone came with me to the Houses of

Parliament this afternoon. Someone who could make a speech."

"Ms Wiz," said Podge.

"No no," said Ms Wiz. "I couldn't possibly. I don't think magic and politics mix."

"Come on," said Jack. "You've taught Class Three. It would be a piece of cake after that."

"Do it for me," begged Podge.

"I think you'd do it very well," said the Prime Minister. "I'll introduce you to the House of Commons and Marjorie can look after Podge and Jack, if you'll just let her move around again."

Ms Wiz sighed. "Oh, all right," she said. "Just a *little* speech."

"Yeah!" said Jack. "Vote for Ms Wiz!"

"Order, order!"

Thirty minutes later, Podge and Jack were looking down on the House of

Commons from a high balcony where they had been taken by Marjorie.

"The government MPs are on one side and the opposition MPs are on the other," Marjorie whispered. "The person in the wig, who keeps saying 'Order, order', is called the Speaker. She's meant to keep everyone under control."

"She's not doing much of a job," muttered Jack. "I've seen more order in the last Assembly of term at St Barnabas."

"But where's the Prime Minister? Where's Ms Wiz?" asked Podge.

As he spoke, an odd growling sound came from the MPs below them. They seemed to be looking towards the door.

"Here they come," said Marjorie.

Slowly the Prime Minister made his way between the rows of MPs. Pale but dignified, Ms Wiz followed him. As they took their seats on the front bench, the Speaker pointed towards them.

"Pray silence for the Prime Minister," she said loudly.

The Prime Minister stood up. "Er, actually," he said, "I'm not going to make a speech this afternoon—"

"Good!" shouted one of the MPs opposite.

"Run out of words, have you?" laughed another.

"How rude," said Podge. "I hope they're not this mean to Ms Wiz."

"Instead, I've asked my good friend Ms Wiz to speak on my behalf."

An astonished silence descended on the chamber.

Ms Wiz rose to her feet. "Thanks, PM," she said. "Now, the reason why I've decided to talk to you this afternoon is that I want you to pass a law to help a boy called Peter Harris."

"Order, order," the Speaker interrupted. "What on earth is going on here? You can't just wander in here and announce that you want to make a law—"

A faint humming sound filled the House of Commons.

"Hoo hoo hoo."

The children stared at the Speaker in amazement. In her place, there now sat a small grey monkey jumping up and down angrily.

One of the MPs on the front bench facing Ms Wiz stood up. "I must object to a complete stranger coming into the House and somehow replacing Madam Speaker with a monkey. This is absolutely . . . whaaaahhhahhhaahhh."

In his place stood a gorilla, thumping his chest.

"Uh-oh," said Jack. "Something tells me Ms Wiz is losing control of this situation."

"Now Peter Harris likes his—" Ms Wiz raised her voice above the noise of interruptions "—he likes his food—". Every MP who stood up to say something was turned into a different kind of monkey.

Soon her words were being drowned by

the noise of chattering, angry, scratching monkeys.

Ms Wiz looked about her and frowned. "We shall return," she said, pulling the Prime Minister to his feet and backing towards the door. "We shall work on our speech at Number Ten, Downing Street."

"I suppose that's it then," said Jack, getting to his feet. "We'd better go home."

Podge followed gloomily. "Ms Wiz was right about one thing," he said. "Politics and magic don't mix."

CHAPTER FOUR

A Message from the PM

The Prime Minister's car moved slowly through the crowds that had gathered outside the Houses of Parliament.

On the back seat Podge and Jack sat between the Prime Minister and Marjorie. Ms Wiz was in the front, waving to the crowd.

"What's happened to Ms Wiz?" Jack whispered to Podge. "One speech to the House of Commons and suddenly she's behaving like she's the Queen or something."

"And it wasn't exactly the greatest speech ever made," grumbled Podge. "We'll never get my dad to change his mind now."

"Cameras, television, that's what you want," said the Prime Minister in a strange, dreamlike voice.

"Oh, Prime Minister—" Ms Wiz smiled modestly. "All this fame – and so soon."

"I meant for Podge," said the Prime Minister. "If we want his parents to change their mind, we'll need publicity. Television."

"That's it!" Jack turned to Podge. "If you appeared on television, your dad would *have* to pay attention. You'd be the week's good cause – Podge-Aid."

"Marjorie, I want to speak to the nation with Ms Wiz," said the Prime Minister suddenly. "In half an hour's time."

"B-but, sir." Marjorie had turned pale. "We're only meant to do that when there's a national emergency."

"This is an emergency. Podge is being forced to leave St Barnabas."

"Anyway," said Marjorie, "it's a terrible time to appear on television – everyone will be waiting to watch that daily soap opera, *The Avenue*."

"Dad's favourite programme!" said Podge.

"Perfect." The Prime Minister smiled. "Get the cameras round as soon as we arrive."

"My speech!" In the front seat, Ms Wiz stopped waving for a moment. "I must work on my speech."

"Crazy," sighed Jack.

Mr Harris was exhausted. He had helped Mrs Harris while she was assembling the desk. He had watched while she tidied all the books in the bedroom. He had stood by, offering advice while Mrs Harris worked out a diet that would help produce a lean, mean Peter Harris.

"Phew," he said, flopping into an armchair in front of the television. "Any chance of a cup of tea, Mother?"

"No, Cuthbert." Mrs Harris sat down beside him. "I made the desk. You make

the tea. There's just time before *The Avenue*."

Grumbling, Mr Harris stood up. "Work, work, work," he muttered.

"I can't think where Peter's got to," said Mrs Harris. "He was meant to be back an hour ago."

"Having too much fun probably," Mr Harris called out from the kitchen. "There'll be an end to that with the new school."

Grumbling, he returned to the sitting room and switched on the television.

"There's now a change to the advertised programme," said the TV announcer. "Instead of *The Avenue*, we'll be going over live in a few moments to Number Ten, Downing Street for a message from the Prime Minister."

"Oh *no!*" said Mr Harris.

The Prime Minister's office was lit up by television lights.

A rather large television producer, called Miss Barkworth, was fussing around with the papers on the Prime Minister's desk. "This is all most irregular, sir," she said. "We haven't even been given a script for you to read from the autocue."

"What's an autocue?" Jack asked Podge as they watched the preparations.

"It's the little screen they read from

when they're making a speech on telly,"
Podge whispered.

"I don't need a script," the Prime
Minister was telling the producer. "My
colleague Ms Wiz will be doing most of the
talking."

"But who is this Wiz person?" The
producer lowered her voice as she saw Ms
Wiz pacing nervously backwards and
forwards in the office. "Has she ever done
any public speaking?"

"She spoke to the House of Commons
this afternoon," said the Prime Minister.
"An excellent speech, it was."

"Yeah," muttered Jack. "She made
monkeys of them."

Ms Wiz stood in front of the mirror,
rehearsing her lines. "Ladies and
gentlemen," she said, then frowned. "No,
too serious . . . Hullo, everybody! No,
that's wrong . . . Hi, my name's Ms Wiz—"

"Just be yourself," smiled Podge. "You'll
be fine."

"Thirty seconds before we're on air," shouted Miss Barkworth, scurrying behind the camera. "I want the PM at his desk, Ms Wiz standing beside him and the fat boy a bit to the left."

"She's not exactly Miss Skinny herself," murmured Jack as he moved out of camera range.

"Sshh!" The producer held up five fingers, then four . . . three . . . two . . . one . . .

The Prime Minister switched on his most sincere smile as a red light appeared above the camera.

"Hullo," he said. "I expect you're all wondering why I decided to speak to the nation this afternoon . . ."

CHAPTER FIVE

A Lady not for Turning

Mr Harris sat grumpily in front of the television set, a mug of tea in his hand.

"Politicians!" he said to Mrs Harris. "You work hard, you do your best for your lad. All you ask in return is the chance to relax in front of *The Avenue*. But no—"

"It must be something really important," said Mrs Harris. "People don't interrupt *The Avenue* for nothing."

"Publicity, Mother." Mr Harris slurped his tea. "Your average politician will do anything for publicity."

"And so," the Prime Minister was saying on television, "I would now like to hand you over to my friend and colleague, Ms Wiz."

"Ms Wiz?" Mr Harris sat forward in his chair. "Isn't that the woman who turned up at St Barnabas and sent a rat up the school inspector's trousers?"

"What on earth is she doing there?" asked Mrs Harris.

"I always knew that woman spelt trouble—"

"Shush, Cuthbert," said Mrs Harris. "Let's hear what she has to say."

Ms Wiz sat easily on the edge of the Prime Minister's desk. "This afternoon I want to tell you the story of a little boy," she said. "Just an ordinary lad. He likes his books. He likes his friends. He likes his chocolate biscuits."

As she smiled, the camera moved closer to her face.

"Yet this little boy's father has decided to drag him away from his school, his lovely childhood friends—"

"Poor little mite," said Mr Harris.

"—his nice stories—"

"What a shame," said Mr Harris.

"—even his chocolate biscuits."

Mr Harris shook his head. "Some parents don't deserve to have children," he said.

"Is this fair?" The woman on the television glanced to her right. "Look at this boy. Is he really so fat?"

She paused as the camera turned to show a child in the shadows of the office.

"Yes, all right, perhaps he is a bit . . . plump," Ms Wiz smiled. "But maybe he eats food as a way of expressing himself, as a way of asking for love from his mum and dad. Maybe every chocolate biscuit that

he eats is not so much a chocolate biscuit as a cry for help—"

"And the little thing looks just like our Peter," sobbed Mrs Harris.

"I don't care who he is." Mr Harris blew his nose on a big red handkerchief. "That boy's parents should be more understanding."

"So I ask you all today," the woman continued, "listen to your children. They have the right to have friends, books – even chocolate biscuits now and then. Let the

example of Podge Harris be an example to us all."

Mr and Mrs Harris stopped crying and stared at one another in amazement.

"Podge Harris?" they said.

The cameras had left Number Ten, Downing Street but Ms Wiz was behaving more and more strangely.

"Where are my ministers?" she asked, looking about her as she sat at the Prime Minister's desk. "I want to go to Parliament and make some laws."

"You did brilliantly, Ms Wiz," said Podge. "But I think we ought to be on our way home. Our parents will be getting worried."

"Home?" Ms Wiz looked shocked. "But my work here has just begun. This lady is not for turning."

"I'm starving," muttered Podge.

"Now, PM—" Ms Wiz beckoned to the

back of the room where the Prime Minister stood with Marjorie and Miss Barkworth. "I'd like to discuss some new laws that we'll be making."

"But Ms Wiz—" The Prime Minister smiled politely. "You've turned most of Parliament into monkeys."

"The spell will have worn off by now," said Ms Wiz. "But I could do it again if you like. Yes, that's a good idea. If people disagree with us, I'll just change them into monkeys."

"What are we going to do with her?" Podge whispered to Jack. "She's gone power-crazy."

Jack was staring at Henry the goldfish, whose plastic bag he had put on a bookshelf nearby. "What we need is a bit of magic to help us. A bit of Henry magic." He picked up the bag. "Oh no, Ms Wiz," he said loudly. "Look what's happened."

Frowning, Ms Wiz turned. "What's the problem, Jack?" she asked.

"It's Henry. He's been dazzled by the television lights." He held the fish up in front of Ms Wiz's eyes. "Ms Wiz," he said, "You want to go . . . to . . . sleep."

Ms Wiz stared straight ahead of her.

Podge gulped. "I don't believe it!" he gasped. "You've hypnotised Ms Wiz."

"She said Henry had his own magic. I thought it might work on her and it did." Jack smiled. "Ms Wiz, you are now going to say goodbye to the Prime Minister," he said.

"Goodbye, Prime Minister," said Ms Wiz in a sleepy voice.

"Goodbye, Ms Wiz," said the Prime Minister.

"You will ask him to pass a law banning all schools."

"Jack!" Podge grabbed his arm. "Don't mess about – let's go home."

"That was a joke, Ms Wiz," said Jack quickly. "Please take us back to the purple dodgem and then fly us home."

"Anything you say, Jack," said Ms Wiz.

They walked slowly towards the front door. "Shouldn't you take the spell off the Prime Minister?" Marjorie asked. "Otherwise he'll be staring into space and talking like a computer for ever."

Jack looked at the Prime Minister for a moment. "I don't think anyone will notice the difference," he said.

"Thanks, PM," Podge shouted back.

"Good luck, Podge," said the Prime Minister, closing the door of Number Ten, Downing Street behind them.

The purple dodgem hovered just above 15 Rylett Road before landing gently on the Harrises' carefully tended lawn.

"Peter!" Mrs Harris opened the front door. "We were so worried about you."

Mr Harris appeared behind his wife. "We saw you on telly, son. You looked great."

"Dad's been thinking," said Mrs Harris, nudging her husband.

"Have I?" Mr Harris frowned. "Oh yes."
He placed his arm around Podge's
shoulder. "Son," he said, "maybe I was a
bit . . . hasty this morning."

"You mean about the books and the
biscuits and St Barnabas?" asked Podge.

"That's right." Mr Harris managed a
smile.

"Yeah," said Jack. "Good old Mr Harris!
And it's all thanks to Ms Wiz."

They turned to the purple dodgem

where Ms Wiz was still sitting motionlessly.

"What's the matter with her, Jack?" asked Mrs Harris.

"I think she's just feeling a bit tired," said Jack, walking over to the dodgem. He clicked his fingers in front of Ms Wiz's eyes.

"Wha – what?" Ms Wiz shook her head and rubbed her eyes, as if she were just waking up. "I had this weird dream that I went crazy for power."

"Unbelievable," said Jack.

"And—" Ms Wiz started laughing, "I even thought Podge was being taken away from St Barnabas and put on a diet."

"Ridiculous," said Mr Harris.

"Oh well, so long as it was just a dream," said Ms Wiz. "I'd better get this back to the fair." There was a faint humming noise as she drove the purple dodgem back to the road. "I think I'll go by road to the fairground," she said. "The traffic isn't too bad."

"Drive carefully, Ms Wiz," said Podge.
"And thank you."

"Bye, Podge. Bye, Jack," she called out.
"Bye, Mr and Mrs Harris."

With a roar of the engine, she accelerated
away and within seconds had turned the
corner of the street and disappeared. For a
moment, Mr and Mrs Harris and the
children listened as the scream of tyres
faded in the distance.

"She may be magic but she's no driver,"
muttered Mr Harris.

Podge turned into the house. "I'm starving," he said.

"Oh, Peter," said Mrs Harris.

"What about that diet then, son?" Mr Harris asked.

"Podge." Jack stepped forward, holding Henry the goldfish in front of him. "Watch the fishy, please."

Podge hesitated, then followed Henry with his eyes as he swam round and round.

"Can you hear me?" said Jack.

"Yeees." Podge's voice was strange and lifeless. "I can hear you, O master."

"Say after me – I want to go . . . to . . . sleep."

"I want . . . I want . . . I want . . . I want a chocolate biscuit."

Jack shrugged at Mr and Mrs Harris as Podge made for the kitchen.

"Sometimes the magic takes a little time to work," he said.